TREVOR ZEGRAS

HOCKEY SUPERSTAR

BY ROY RATHBURN

Book design by Jake Nordby
Cover design by Jake Nordby

Photographs ©: Kyusung Gong/AP Images, cover, 1; Jeffrey T. Barnes/AP Images, 4, 30; Bill Wippert/NHLI/Getty Images, 7; Tim Clayton/Corbis Sport/Getty Images, 8; Russell Hons/Cal Sport Media/ZUMA Wire/AP Images, 11; Maddie Meyer/Getty Images Sport/Getty Images, 12–13; Codie McLachlan/Getty Images Sport/Getty Images, 14, 16–17; Rick Scuteri/AP Images, 19; Alex Gallardo/AP Images, 20–21; Ethan Miller/Getty Images Sport/Getty Images, 22, 25; Bruce Bennett/Getty Images Sport/Getty Images, 26; Red Line Editorial, 29

Press Box Books, an imprint of Press Room Editions, Inc.

ISBN
978-1-63494-877-7 (library bound)
978-1-63494-895-1 (paperback)
978-1-63494-929-3 (epub)
978-1-63494-913-2 (hosted ebook)

Library of Congress Control Number: 2023923320

Distributed by North Star Editions, Inc.
2297 Waters Drive
Mendota Heights, MN 55120
www.northstareditions.com

Printed in the United States of America
082024

About the Author

Roy Rathburn is a retired English teacher and former hockey player, coach, and official, from northern Minnesota.

TABLE OF CONTENTS

UCI Health
46
BAUER
46
BAUER
BAUER
BAUER
BAUER

1 SOMETHING NEW

Trevor Zegras settled behind the opponent's net with the puck on his stick. The Anaheim Ducks center looked over his options. His teammates drove toward the net looking for a pass.

Zegras waited. Being behind the net gives a player lots of opportunities. It forces the defense to react. And the goaltender can't see the puck.

Zegras's teammate Sonny Milano stood in front of the goal. Meanwhile, a Buffalo Sabres defender charged behind

Trevor Zegras lifts the puck during a December 2021 game against the Buffalo Sabres.

the net to chase after Zegras. Then Zegras surprised everyone in the arena. He whipped his stick blade around, lifting the puck into the air. Then he tossed the puck over the net toward Milano. While the puck was in midair, Milano jabbed at it. He knocked it into the goal. The goalie had no idea what had happened.

Even Zegras couldn't believe it. He put his hands on his head in disbelief. Zegras couldn't help but watch the replay on the scoreboard to see how he'd pulled it off.

Fans could never take their eyes off a player like Zegras. He was capable of

A LEGEND IS BORN

Trevor Zegras's play was a first in hockey. Fans began calling it the Zegras. Other players started trying to do a Zegras themselves. Even gamers tried to recreate the play in the *NHL 22* video game. The game's maker ended up including it as a special move in the 2023 edition of the game.

Zegras reacts to his amazing assist to Sonny Milano.

amazing moments. This goal was one of many eye-popping plays he'd made since entering the National Hockey League (NHL).

11
BAUER
JR
11
CCM
21
BAUER
11
MF
BAUER

2 STRIVING FOR GREATNESS

Trevor Zegras was born on March 20, 2001, in Bedford, New York. When he was growing up, Trevor played many different sports. But there was something special about hockey. Trevor loved the feeling of skating on the ice.

Trevor began skating when he was three years old. On top of playing hockey, Trevor also loved watching the sport. He and his family were big fans of the New York Rangers. But Trevor's favorite player was Patrick Kane of the

Trevor Zegras (11) tries to gain control of the puck during a Pee Wee game in 2014.

Chicago Blackhawks. Kane was known for his fancy stickhandling and highlight-reel goals. Trevor wanted to be the same kind of player. As a kid, he loved practicing his skills wherever he could. He stickhandled throughout the house. In the driveway, he tried shots behind his back.

Trevor's extra practice showed on the ice. As a 15-year-old, he averaged more than a point per game. For his next step, Trevor wanted to play for USA Hockey's National Team Development Program (NTDP), just like Kane had done.

NHL FRIENDS

Trevor Zegras enjoys a close friendship with Jack Hughes of the New Jersey Devils. The two have known each other since childhood. And they became good friends while playing for the NTDP. They were both selected in the first round of the 2019 draft. While the Ducks were out of the NHL playoffs in 2023, Trevor went to the Devils' playoff games to support his friend.

Trevor Zegras first played for the US junior national team in 2017.

In the spring of 2017, Trevor attended a camp for the NTDP. His excitement was through the roof when he found out he made the team. In his first year with the NTDP, he totaled 59 points in 56 games. In his second and final year, he recorded 87 points in 60 games. A true playmaker, Trevor had more than twice as many assists as goals.

The 2018–19 NTDP team featured a ton of stars. Future NHL players Jack Hughes, Cole Caufield, and Alex Turcotte were some of Trevor's teammates. In fact, eight players on the team were chosen in the first round of the 2019 NHL Entry Draft. The Anaheim Ducks drafted Trevor with the ninth pick that year.

But Trevor wasn't heading to the NHL right away. He had committed to Boston University to play at least one year of college hockey. Trevor stood out as one of the best freshmen in the country. He averaged more than a point per game. There wasn't much left for Trevor to prove. After one year, he left college to turn pro.

Trevor Zegras tallied 36 points in 33 games in his one year at Boston University.

Bank
BAUER
HOCKEY EAST
BOSTON
13
CCM

CHIPOTLE
BAUER
USA
BAUER

3 AMERICAN HERO

Trevor Zegras signed his first professional contract in March 2020. However, his pro hockey debut had to wait. All professional hockey leagues were on pause at the time because of the COVID-19 pandemic. Zegras still played big-time hockey in 2020, though. He was young enough to play for Team USA in the World Junior Championship.

So, that December, Zegras joined some of the best American players age 20 and under. In the previous year's

In his first World Junior Championship, Zegras recorded nine assists in five games.

tournament, he had led all players with nine assists. But Zegras dominated even more the second time around.

Zegras led Team USA all the way to the gold-medal game. Going into that contest, he was tied for the tournament lead in total points. Now, Team USA would be taking on Canada. The mighty Canadians were on home ice. They hadn't lost a single game in the tournament. But Zegras believed Team USA was prepared to shock them.

An assist from Zegras helped put Team USA ahead 1–0 in the first period. The assist gave Zegras the scoring lead in the tournament. And he wasn't done. In the second period, Zegras took control of the puck near the net.

Zegras scans the ice during the gold-medal game of the 2021 World Junior Championship.

CHIPOTLE
BAUER
TELUS
9
17
McMICHAEL

He surprised the Canadian goalie with a quick backhanded shot to double Team USA's lead. The Americans held on to upset Canada and win gold.

Zegras then made his pro hockey debut with the minor league San Diego Gulls on February 5, 2021. In a 10-minute span, he scored a goal and had two assists.

After a little more than two weeks, the Anaheim Ducks called up Zegras. He made his NHL debut on February 22 against the Arizona Coyotes. The Ducks had high hopes for Zegras. But he got off to a slow start. He didn't score

WORLD JUNIOR LEGEND

Zegras scored 27 total points in his two appearances at the World Junior Championship. He tied Jordan Schroeder for the all-time record among American players. Schroeder had set the record in 2010. However, Zegras scored all his points in just 12 games. It took Schroeder 19 games.

Zegras recorded two shots on goal in his NHL debut.

his first goal until March 18. But he finished the season strong, tallying points in six of his last eight games.

After that, Zegras returned to the Gulls. The Ducks wanted him to keep working. They also wanted him to try moving from wing to center. When Zegras came back to the Ducks, they expected it to be for good.

MORE TO COME

Trevor Zegras was patient for his first NHL goal. He received a pass close to the net. Then he pulled the puck back to make the goalie dive forward. Finally, Zegras ripped the puck into the back of the open net.

ZEGRAS
46

BAUER

4 FLYING HIGH

The move to center worked well for Trevor Zegras. He started scoring more with the Gulls. And he played a more complete game. When opening night of the 2021–22 NHL season rolled around, the Ducks named Zegras their top center.

Wherever Zegras was on the ice, he made an impact. He clicked right away with linemates Sonny Milano and Rickard Rakell. His lacrosse-style assist to Milano was an early highlight of his NHL career.

Zegras scored 23 goals in his first full NHL season.

Zegras racked up 25 points in his first 30 games of the season.

Zegras started to get some consideration for the 2022 All-Star Game. He didn't end up making the team. But he did take part in the Breakaway Challenge on All-Star weekend. Zegras scored one-on-one against a goalie while he wore a blindfold.

Before long, Zegras started showing up on highlight reels everywhere. Against Montreal, Zegras picked up the puck with his stick again. But this time, he wasn't looking to pass. Zegras whipped the puck into the net by himself. Only

TV STAR

Trevor Zegras made his acting debut in 2022. He appeared in an episode of *The Mighty Ducks: Game Changers* with teammates Troy Terry and Max Jones. The show is about a youth hockey team. In one episode, the team practices at the Anaheim Ducks' arena. Zegras, Terry, and Jones join the kids for practice.

Zegras competes blindfolded in the 2022 Breakaway Challenge.

a few players have been able to score goals this way in the NHL. And later that year, Zegras did it again.

Zegras recorded more than 60 points in each of his first two full seasons in the NHL.

Zegras scored in other ways, too. He finished the season with 23 goals and 38 assists. Those numbers put him second on the Ducks in scoring that season. He was also a finalist for the Calder Trophy. That award goes to the league's best rookie each season.

Zegras became the Ducks' top scorer in 2022–23. And he had no shortage of exciting plays. In a game against the Seattle Kraken, Zegras received a pass as he streaked toward the goal. He pulled the puck back through his own legs. Then he instantly fired a shot as the goalie struggled to track the puck. The goal was so good that it even amazed the opposing fans.

The Ducks knew they had a superstar to build their team around for years to come. Before the 2023–24 season, Zegras signed a new three-year contract. That meant Anaheim fans could look forward to many more amazing plays. But there was one thrill Zegras hadn't yet provided. Up to that point, he hadn't led Anaheim to the playoffs. Going on a deep playoff run would be his greatest trick yet.

TIMELINE

1. **Bedford, New York (March 20, 2001)**
   Trevor Zegras is born.

2. **Vancouver, British Columbia (June 21, 2019)**
   The Anaheim Ducks choose Zegras ninth overall in the NHL Entry Draft.

3. **Boston, Massachusetts (March 7, 2020)**
   Zegras plays his final game with Boston University.

4. **Edmonton, Alberta (January 5, 2021)**
   Zegras has an assist and a goal in Team USA's 2–0 win over Canada in the gold-medal game of the World Junior Championship.

5. **Glendale, Arizona (February 22, 2021)**
   Zegras makes his NHL debut against the Arizona Coyotes.

6. **Anaheim, California (March 18, 2021)**
   In a game against the Coyotes, Zegras scores his first NHL goal.

7. **Buffalo, New York (December 7, 2021)**
   Zegras uses a lacrosse-style pass to assist a Sonny Milano goal. The play quickly becomes famous throughout the hockey world.

8. **Seattle, Washington (March 7, 2023)**
   Zegras scores a goal through his own legs in a game against the Seattle Kraken.

MAP

AT A GLANCE

Birth date: March 20, 2001

Birthplace: Bedford, New York

Position: Center

Shoots: Left

Size: 6 feet (183 cm), 185 pounds (84 kg)

NHL team: Anaheim Ducks (2021-)

Previous teams: San Diego Gulls (2021), Boston University (2019–20)

Major awards: World Junior Championship MVP (2021), NHL All-Rookie Team (2022)

Accurate through the 2022–23 season.

GLOSSARY

assists
Passes, rebounds, or deflections that result in goals.

center
A forward who typically plays in the middle of the offensive zone.

contract
A written agreement that keeps a player with a team for a certain amount of time.

debut
First appearance.

draft
An event that allows teams to choose new players coming into the league.

freshmen
Students in their first year.

linemates
Defensemen or forwards that a player typically is paired with while on the ice.

pro
Short for professional; getting paid to play.

rookie
A first-year player.

upset
To unexpectedly win a game against a supposedly better team.

TO LEARN MORE

Books

Berglund, Bruce. *Hockey GOATs: The Greatest Athletes of All Time*. North Mankato, MN: Capstone Press, 2024.

Clarke, David J. *Anaheim Ducks*. Mendota Heights, MN: Press Box Books, 2023.

Wiseman, Blaine. *Stanley Cup*. New York: Lightbox Learning, 2024.

More Information

To learn more about Trevor Zegras, go to **pressboxbooks.com/AllAccess**.

These links are routinely monitored and updated to provide the most current information available.

INDEX